D0116232

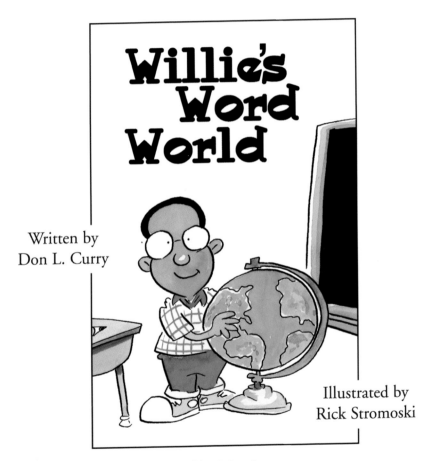

Willie's Word World

Written by
Don L. Curry

Illustrated by
Rick Stromoski

Children's Press®
A Division of Scholastic Inc.
New York • Toronto • London • Auckland • Sydney
Mexico City • New Delhi • Hong Kong
Danbury, Connecticut

Dear Parents/Educators,

Welcome to Rookie Ready to Learn. Each Rookie Reader in this series includes additional age-appropriate Let's Learn Together activity pages that help your young child to be better prepared when starting school. *Willie's Word World* offers opportunities for you and your child to talk about the important social/emotional skill of **self-awareness**.

Here are early-learning skills you and your child will encounter in the *Willie's Word World* Let's Learn Together pages:

• Math: adding on

• Recognizing letters

We hope you enjoy sharing this delightful, enhanced reading experience with your early learner.

Library of Congress Cataloging-in-Publication Data

Curry, Don L.
  Willie's word world / written by Don L. Curry ; illustrated by Rick Stromoski.
     p. cm. -- (Rookie ready to learn)
  Summary: Willie and his classmates create alliterative sentences based on their names. Includes suggested learning activities.
  ISBN 978-0-531-26374-7 – 978-0-531-26679-3 (pbk.)
  [1. Alliteration--Fiction. 2. English language--Phonetics--Fiction. 3. Alphabet--Fiction.] I. Stromoski, Rick, ill. II. Title. III. Series.
  PZ7.C93595Wi 2011
  [E]--dc22

                            2010050004

1 2 3 4 5 6 7 8 9 10 R 18 17 16 15 14 13 12 11

My name is Willie. I love words.

Today, Mrs. Walters wanted to play a word game. We had to make up silly sentences.

The words in the sentences
had to start with the
first letter of our names.

"Skinny swans swim secretly seaward," Sarah said.

What words start with W?

"Little Lucy licks a lizard lollipop," Lincoln said.

"Dizzy dolphins dive down deep," Danny said.

What words start with W? Willie thought.

"Rats read recipes for rock soup," Ray said.

"Cockroaches can't carry candy covered carrots," Connor said.

What words start with W?

"Al's apples have baby alligators in them," Ali said.

"Pretty pigs eat peppermints
with penguins," Patricia said.

What words start with W?

"Ten toads tickle tiny tarantula toes," Tommy said.

"Big bubbles bounced like balls on the beach," said Brendan.

What words start with W?

"Chickens chased chunky chipmunks," Charlie said.

I need words with W!

"Walruses water-ski over the waterfall in the winter!" Willie yelled.

Wow!

31

Congratulations!

You just finished reading *Willie's Word World* and learned about being brave.

About the Author
Don L. Curry is a writer, editor, and educational consultant who lives and works in New York City.

About the Illustrator
Rick Stromoski is a self-taught cartoonist and humorous illustrator. His work has appeared in national magazines, children's and humor books, newspapers, licensed products, national advertising, and on network television.

Willie's Word World

Let's learn together!

Five Brave Firefighters

Willie thinks firefighters are brave.

Five brave firefighters,
(Hold up five fingers.)

Sleeping so.
(Lower fingers flat across palm.)

The fire bell rings,
(Open up your hand.)

Down the pole they go.
(Make a downward motion with your hand.)

Jump in the fire truck. Hurry down the street. Climb up the ladder.
(Make your fingers climb.)

Feel the fire's heat.
(Wipe sweat from your brow.)

Five brave firefighters,
(Hold up five fingers.)

Put the fire out.
(Make a wiping motion)

Hip! Hip! Hooray!
All the people shout!
(Shout.)

PARENT TIP: Much of the time, we associate bravery with high-risk adult activities such as being a firefighter, serving in the military, or overcoming an adversity or challenge. However, children often have to be brave to get a medical shot, sleep in a new place, or meet new people. Pointing out and talking about acts of courage and bravery during our everyday activities helps encourage the act and deepens understanding of the concept.

How Many More?

Mrs. Walters needs more pencils and books. The students want to help her get them. Have a grown-up help you read each question. Point to the answer.

Mrs. Walters has one book. She needs three. How many more books does Sarah need to get for Mrs. Walters?

Mrs. Walters has two pencils. She needs five. How many more pencils does Willie need to get for Mrs. Walters?

What's the Word?

Say the missing words to complete the silly sentences.

1. Three rats went to the _____
   place

   to get rocks for their recipe.

2. The school bus pulled up and a fuzzy

   _____ was driving!
   animal

3. The _____ ball bounced so high
   color

   that it almost reached the airplane!

4. Two delightful dogs opened the restaurant

   menu and chose _____ to eat.
   food

W Is Wonderful!

Wow! Willie loves words! The words below all start with *W*.

Name each picture. Then point to the correct word that goes with the picture.

wagon

watch

whale

window

Willie and his friends love to create silly sentences.

Most of the words in their sentences started with the first letter of their names. What letter does your name start with? What words start with that letter? Make up your own silly sentence.

PARENT TIP: When words in a sentence start with the same letter, it is called *alliteration*. (You might remember the traditional rhyme of "Sally sells seashells by the seashore.") Repeating the same sound at the beginning of different words helps your child learn to listen carefully for the beginning sounds in words.

Animal Alphabet

Willie, Danny, and Ali are looking for their favorite animals.
Each child's name begins with the same letter as his or her
favorite animal's name. Use your finger to trace the path
that leads each child to his or her favorite animal.

Ali

dolphin

Danny

walrus

Willie

alligator

Willie's Word World Word List (107 Words)

a	dizzy	of	ten
Al's	dolphins	on	the
Ali	down	our	them
alligators	eat	over	thought
apples	first	Patricia	tickle
baby	for	penguins	tiny
balls	game	peppermints	to
beach	had	pigs	toads
big	have	play	today
bounced	I	pretty	toes
Brendan	in	rats	Tommy
bubbles	is	Ray	up
candy	letter	read	walruses
can't	licks	recipes	Walters
carrots	like	rock	wanted
carry	Lincoln	said	waterfall
Charlie	little	Sarah	water-ski
chased	lizard	seaward	we
chickens	lollipop	secretly	what
chipmunks	love	sentences	Willie
chunky	Lucy	silly	winter
cockroaches	make	skinny	with
Connor	Mrs.	soup	word
covered	my	start	words
Danny	name	swans	wow
deep	names	swim	yelled
dive	need	tarantula	

PARENT TIP: Have more fun with words and alliteration. With your child, look at the word list and write down all the animal names. Invite your child to give each animal a name using the same letter that begins the animal's name, such as Priscilla the Penguin.

40